Samuel French Acting Edition

My Big Gay Italian Christmas

by Anthony Wilkinson

FOR PRODUCTION ENQUIRIES

UNITED STATES AND CANADA
info@concordtheatricals.com
1-866-979-0447

UNITED KINGDOM AND EUROPE
licensing@concordtheatricals.co.uk
020-7054-7200

Each title is subject to availability from Concord Theatricals Corp., depending upon country of performance. Please be aware that *MY BIG GAY ITALIAN CHRISTMAS* may not be licensed by Concord Theatricals Corp. in your territory. Professional and amateur producers should contact the nearest Concord Theatricals Corp. office or licensing partner to verify availability.

system, or transmitted in any form, by any means, now known or yet to be invented, including mechanical, electronic, photocopying, recording, videotaping, or otherwise, without the prior written permission of the publisher. No one shall upload this title(s), or part of this title(s), to any social media websites.

For all enquiries regarding motion picture, television, and other media rights, please contact Concord Theatricals Corp.

MUSIC USE NOTE

Licensees are solely responsible for obtaining formal written permission from copyright owners to use copyrighted music in the performance of this play and are strongly cautioned to do so. If no such permission is obtained by the licensee, then the licensee must use only original music that the licensee owns and controls. Licensees are solely responsible and liable for all music clearances and shall indemnify the copyright owners of the play(s) and their licensing agent, Concord Theatricals Corp., against any costs, expenses, losses and liabilities arising from the use of music by licensees. Please contact the appropriate music licensing authority in your territory for the rights to any incidental music.

IMPORTANT BILLING AND CREDIT REQUIREMENTS

If you have obtained performance rights to this title, please refer to your licensing agreement for important billing and credit requirements.

MY BIG GAY ITALIAN CHRISTMAS was first produced by Bianco Productions in Atlantic City, New Jersey at the Golden Nugget Hotel & Casino. The play had its first preview on December 2nd, 2017. The production was directed by Sonia Blangiardo and general managed by 22Q Entertainment. The Production Stage Managers were Robert Levinstein and Teresa Anne Cicala. The Technical Director was Ray Adler and the Director of Operations was Deanna Fooks. The cast was as follows:

ANTHONY . . . . Anthony J. Wilkinson
TONIANN . . . . Debra Toscano
ANGELA . . . . Gina Scarda
OLIVIA . . . . Kim Pirrella
JOSEPHINE . . . . Maryann Maisano
VICTORIO . . . . Mark Corallo
MARIA . . . . Elena Barone
SISTER FABIANA . . . . Angelina Malerba
SISTER FONZINA . . . . Janet Malpeso
OFFICER . . . . Mayor John E. McCormac

CHARACTERS

(In order of appearance)
F 8, M 2

ANGELA PINNUNZIATO – Female, late 50's or 60's. Over the top and overbearing Italian Mother. Comedic Actress. Lead

AUNT TONIANN – Female, late 40's or 50's. Eccentric Italian-American woman with lots of attitude and absolutely no filter. Comedic Actress. Lead

MARIA – Female, late 20's or early 30's. Anthony's younger, nine-months pregnant, and very emotionally unstable sister. Supporting

JOSEPHINE – Female, 40's or 50's. Angela and Toniann's first cousin who is a neurotic hypochondria and always the barer of bad news. A very unassuming lesbian. Supporting

ANTHONY PINNUNZIATO – Male, late 30's or 40's. Our Everyman. Stereotypical Italian-American boy next door type. Lead

VICTORIO – Male, late 30's or 40's. A distinguished and very handsome educated doctor, who can win over every gay man and every family that comes with him. Supporting

OLIVIA – Female, late 30's or 40's. An Italian-American ball of fire who is not to be messed with. Lead

OFFICER KELLY GARDNER – Female, Any age. A no nonsense Staten Island cop who is in no mood for games. Supporting

SISTER FONZINA – Female, any age. A kind, pure and caring Italian nun. Supporting

SISTER FABIANA – Female, any Age. Fonzina's less kind and much less pure sister who has no business being in a habit. Supporting

SETTING

Angela Pinnunziato's Staten Island Home

TIME

December 25, 2018

AUTHOR'S NOTE

The bonds made in the arts create families sometimes closer to our own. I dedicate this show to it's original director and sister I never had, Sonia Blangiardo. Her constant support, wisdom and guidance has been a driving force in my creative and personal journey. She has been a blessing in my life and I am forever grateful.

*(Open on **ANGELA**'s living room early afternoon on Christmas Day. The room is decorated appropriately for Christmas with a tree and gifts under it somewhere on stage. A projector or screen if possible can show a table decorated for twenty in the living room and we can assume the kitchen and bedrooms are off stage. **ANGELA** is sitting on the couch with the remote alone, anxiously watching the news as the largest snow storm in Staten Island history approaches.)*

NEWS ANCHOR. *(Voice over.)* We have more breaking news coming in with the snow storm of the century quickly approaching the tri-state area. Over ten thousand flights have been cancelled across the country leaving millions of people incapable of making it home this Christmas. We have just been informed that all of Staten Island, Brooklyn and Central Jersey have been placed on high alert and the mayor has declared a state of emergency for all of New York City. Everyone please stay off the roads and do not put your life or anyone else's lives at risk. You asked for a white Christmas well you got one…this is Ron Corning live with ABC news, Carmela back to you.

ANGELA. SHIT!!!

*(**TONIANN** comes barreling into the house bundled up and in a state of panic with a tray of cookies in hand.)*

TONIANN. Holy Shit Angela! Thank God I made it! I ran around my house in panic and hurried so I could get here as soon as possible before the storm got too bad.

ANGELA. Toniann you live four blocks away you could of walked if it got that bad.

TONIANN. Walked!? Are you watching the news!? We are getting more than twenty inches of snow with fifty mile per hour winds! Is anyone else here yet?

ANGELA. Please, I'm a nervous wreck! Maria and Howie should be here any second, I told her to hurry up.

TONIANN. She can't be on the road nine months pregnant!!

ANGELA. I know please my nerves! I told her to hurry up and I already took two xanax!

TONIANN. What about Peter and Dominick did they make it in?

ANGELA. Nope! Peter called this morning flight was cancelled.

I'm devastated!

TONIANN. Are you fucking kidding me!? I waited online at the Shop Rite for four hours to make his god damn toll house cookies and he's not here!?

ANGELA. Really Toniann!?

TONIANN. Ugh! Well Cousin Josephine will eat them she eats everything in sight anyway.

ANGELA. No she won't, you didn't get the email from her!? She's on a new "Farm to Table" diet to lose weight. If it's not from the farm she can't eat it.

TONIANN. Oh please Angela with her and her fucking diets. It's a holiday and we all have to watch *her* figure. Please! I'm over her shit!

ANGELA. You!? I had to design a whole menu just for her.

TONIANN. Of course you did! You're way better than me! I would of told her to stay home or go to a farm if that's her new thing.

Ya know she's just like Aunt Rosie! Complains and complains about everything!

ANGELA. Oh I know! Please all I want is my kids safe for the holiday.

Anthony made it in thankfully so he should be here soon too.

Did you hear about the new doctor?!

TONIANN. He has a new doctor!? What's wrong with him?

ANGELA. No!! He has a new boyfriend!! And he is a doctor... Victorio!

TONIANN. I talk to him every day at work, how come I don't know about this!?

ANGELA. He said he doesn't want to jinx it so he didn't tell anyone.

TONIANN. Victorio! Oh My God an Italian doctor! I'm so happy for him.

Maybe this will finally help him get over Andrew.

ANGELA. Well if he screws this up and moves back to Santa Fe for Andrew

I'll kill him! Look at the flower arrangement Victorio sent...

(**ANGELA** *shows* **TONIANN** *the arrangement.*)

TONIANN. Oh My God that centerpiece is gorgeous!!!

(**TONIANN** *reads the card.*)

"Merry Christmas to the Pinnunziato family, thank you for having me I look forward to meeting you. Victorio Buccatini."

Oh my God the name alone I want to pinch his cheeks!

(**MARIA** *comes barreling in nine months pregnant with a bag of gifts and clearly uncomfortable.* **ANGELA** *and* **TONIANN** *rush to help her.*)

Maria! What are you doing carrying that bag by yourself!?

ANGELA. Where is Howie?!

MARIA. He had to go visit his Mom in the nursing home, he will be here later.

ANGELA. What!!? In Brooklyn!? Maria he won't make it! The storm is getting worse! You drove here by yourself!? Are you crazy!?

MARIA. I took an uber.

TONIANN. Nine months pregnant and he made you take an uber!!?

I'll kill this fuck!!

MARIA. Aunt Toniann please!

ANGELA. Does Howie have my Grandson!?

MARIA. Of course Mom!

TONIANN. He took baby Jonah to Brooklyn in a snow storm!?

Has your husband lost his mind!?

ANGELA. Can we not stress out Maria!? The last thing I need is her getting stressed right now.

MARIA. Mom, I had Cousin Josephine in the grab bag, is she still coming?

ANGELA. Of course. She called me four times to tell me she is on her way and updated me on the storm.

TONIANN. I know, she thinks she's a weather expert that one!

What did you buy her Maria?

MARIA. I got her fifty dollars in casino chips to the Golden Nugget for when she goes to Atlantic City.

TONIANN. Perfect gift for her, she practically lives there. I'll guarantee she has me in the grab bag and she got me that same fuckin Dunkin' Donuts gift card she always gets me. I have been telling her for years I don't even like Dunkin' Donuts, I drink Starbucks!!

ANGELA. Please Toniann can you try to not...

> (**JOSEPHINE** *enters dramatically bag in hands and out of breath.*)

JOSEPHINE. Anthony!! Peter! Somebody help me with the bags!

Ugh! I'm out of breath.

MARIA. Let me help you Josephine.

TONIANN. Maria sit down, Josephine get in here before you catch pneumonia!

JOSEPHINE. Please I had it twice already this year!

I'm telling you Toniann I think Jesus drove my car here.

ANGELA. What do you mean it's not even that bad yet!?

JOSEPHINE. Let me tell you what happened to me! So I'm driving down Hylan Boulevard this morning to fill up my car with gas because I know it's gonna be an issue with this storm and sure enough I pull up to the gas station and roll down the window and I see the name tag on the gas attendant. Joseph!!! Angela... that was my father and your husband coming to us on Christmas!

ANGELA. Oh my God Josephine! I'm gonna cry...

(They hug and **TONIANN** *shoots an eye roll to* **MARIA**.*)*

JOSEPHINE. Oh my God Angela make it louder! Ron Corning is breaking in again.

*(***ANGELA*** grabs the remote and makes the TV louder.)*

NEWS ANCHOR. *(Voice over.)* Reporting now on the latest on what meteorologists are calling the "Whiteout Christmas." Winds have been raised to over sixty miles per hour as we approach the afternoon and we are anticipating the entire tri-state area to be shut down in a state of emergency.

If you are spending Christmas with family you should bring clothes because you will not be able to leave this evening. The Mayor is urging everyone to be off the roads in the next hour. All roads have been declared dangerous and life threatening. Carmela I can only hope that viewers understand how serious this storm is...

*(***ANTHONY*** enters.)*

ANTHONY. Madonna Mia the traffic on Arthur Kill Road!!

TONIANN. Anthony, Thank God you're here!

ANGELA. Where is Victorio?!

ANTHONY. He's parking the car around the block he wanted to allow room for them to plow.

TONIANN. Oh my God a doctor and a saint! I love him already!!

JOSEPHINE / MARIA. Victorio?

Who is Victorio?

ANGELA. Victorio Buccatini. DOCTOR Victorio Buccatini!

Anthony has a new boyfriend.

MARIA. Get out!! Why didn't you tell me this!?

ANTHONY. I know I know, I only told Mom last week, it's just one of those things I didn't want to jinx. I've had the worst luck with men since Andrew and I am just hoping this is finally the one.

JOSEPHINE. He sounds perfect Anthony! I know the whole family!

ANTHONY. You know his family!?

JOSEPHINE. Yes! I grew up with Frankie Buccatini in Bensonhurst. We went to school together. How much do you want to bet that's his father?

TONIANN. It's a common name Josephine.

JOSEPHINE. No it's not!

(**VICTORIO** *enters.*)

VICTORIO. Merry Christmas everyone!

TONIANN. Oh my God he's gorgeous!!

ANTHONY. Everyone allow me to introduce you to my new boyfriend, Victorio.

ANGELA. DOCTOR Victorio.

ANTHONY. MA!

JOSEPHINE. So what kind of doctor are you Victorio?

VICTORIO. I'm actually a heart surgeon.

TONIANN. Of course you are. Why can't I be a gay man?

ANGELA. What can I get you to drink Victorio?

VICTORIO. Oh I'm fine...

ANTHONY. I have it Mom. This is my Mom... Angela, my Aunt Toniann, my Cousin Josephine and my sister Maria.

VICTORIO. Well I see someone is getting ready to have a baby.

TONIANN. My God he's good!!

VICTORIO. When are you due Maria?

MARIA. I'm actually not due till January fifth.

VICTORIO. And Anthony tells me this is your second…

MARIA. Yes! My son Jonah is two now. He is with my husband Howie in Fort Lee visiting his Father.

ANGELA. I thought he was visiting his mother in Brooklyn!?

MARIA. He's doing both.

JOSEPHINE. Is he nuts!? He shouldn't have a baby on the road in this storm.

Angela call him up and tell him what Ron Corning said on the news.

*(**ANGELA** goes to look for her phone.)*

MARIA. NO! Mom please, Howie is well aware what is going on and he knows if it gets bad to stay put where he is. If he can't make it, he can'tmake it!

ANGELA. What!!?? He has my grandson! I want to see my grandson for Christmas!!

MARIA. Well he needed to see his parents Mom.

ANGELA. That selfish fuck! What the hell did he need to see his parents on Christmas for, they're Jews!

ANTHONY. MA!

ANGELA. I'm sorry Victorio, forgive my language my daughter married a Rabbi.

ANTHONY. Is anyone hungry, I'm starving! Anything to pick on?

ANGELA. Yes baby, go inside and get the rice balls and bring them in here while we wait for everyone else.

JOSEPHINE. No one else is gonna make it here I'm telling you Angela! This storm is way worse than they know. My whole life I've never seen anything this bad.

ANGELA. Well your brother and Dominick aren't coming they are stuck in Miami.

ANTHONY. Awwwww...so sad. Rice ball?

ANGELA. Cousin Geraldine and all her kids are stuck in Long Island from last night. I invited Donna Marco and her sister Angel but they are stuck in Toms River and staying with Joey Pirrella's family.

> (**ANTHONY** *offers Cousin* **JOSEPHINE** *a rice ball.)*

JOSEPHINE. Oh no thank you Anthony, I'm on a special farm to table diet so I can't have that.

ANTHONY. Oh I'm sorry, I didn't know.

ANGELA. Josephine, you can have that. It's gluten free rice and I used fresh Ricotta and mozzarella from Pastosa!

JOSEPHINE. That's not farm to table Angela. Don't you agree Victorio that the best way to prevent cancer is a farm to table diet?

VICTORIO. Well it definitely helps, but it is a holiday so you can treat yourself...

TONIANN. Exactly!! Thank you Victorio!!

JOSEPHINE. Well I have been off for years now and it's time to catch up to reality.

No rice balls for me Anthony. What's on the menu for dinner Angela?

ANGELA. I did a farm to table vegetable lasagna just for you and regular lasagna for the rest of us.

JOSEPHINE. Angela!! Lasagna is not farm to table!!

ANGELA. It's vegetables! You said you could have all vegetables!

JOSEPHINE. It's with pasta!!

TONIANN. Pasta is farm to table! Doctor Oz said it helps your metabolism.

You're fine.

VICTORIO. Well, I don't know if I agree with Doctor Oz on that one.

JOSEPHINE. Thank You Victorio! My family is delusional.

VICTORIO. It's a holiday Josephine, enjoy! This brings me back to when my Mother made Lasagna for us on Christmas Day.

JOSEPHINE. Oh you're Italian!?

TONIANN. Victorio Buccatini?! No he's Norwegian Josephine!

Did your mother pass Victorio?

VICTORIO. She is actually in a nursing home. I was there last night for Christmas Eve. She loves to read but she really can't no more so I sat up and read "A Tale Of Two Cities" for her and brought her a beautiful dish of all seven fishes that she can enjoy.

MARIA. Awwwww...that's beautiful!

JOSEPHINE. Did you bring her Christmas cookies too I hope!

VICTORIO. Of course! I bake them every year for her! Is there a bathroom I can use?

ANTHONY. Of course, straight that way to the left.

VICTORIO. Thank you Anthony. Excuse me...

(He exits.)

ANGELA. Anthony if you fuck this up, I'll stab you!

TONIANN. The man is a saint!

ANTHONY. See this is why I don't tell you guys anything because now if something happens again it's my fault.

ANGELA. That's not true! Andrew wasn't your fault the second time.

TONIANN. Or the first time!

JOSEPHINE. I loved Andrew! I almost got him something for Christmas.

I feel terrible.

TONIANN. Fuck Andrew Josephine! Anthony, this is exactly what you need!

I told you a million times the right man would come along and look at him, he's perfect! Gorgeous, successful, Italian, good family values...

ANGELA. I'm so happy for you Anthony!

ANTHONY. Calm down please... I don't want to jinx this!

MARIA. How did you two meet Anthony?

ANTHONY. Well we actually met in Dallas. Body Body is opening up huge down there...

TONIANN. I knew you were gone way too long on these trips! I should've known a man was involved.

ANTHONY. I happened to be very busy but managed to find some time for some fun one night.

JOSEPHINE. So what was HE doing in Dallas?

ANTHONY. He was asked to oversee the development of a new hospital opening up in Waxahachie.

TONIANN. Ok, so how the hell did you two meet?

(**ANTHONY** *comes stage center and begins to tell his story. As he is speaking a bar comes* *out from one end of the stage and the lights slowly dim on the ladies and come up on the bar.)*

ANTHONY. Well I had a free night to myself and the concierge at my hotel told me that I needed to visit this country gay bar in town. So I ubered over and it was so sweet. They had country line dancing and all the guys had cowboy hats on. I was enjoying the music and about to leave when out of nowhere I spotted this handsome guy at the bar...and I could just tell he wasn't from there.

> *(**VICTORIO** has made his way on the stage and is now dressed in country attire with a cowboy hat. He is poised at the bar with a drink. **ANTHONY** makes his way over to **VICTORIO** as the lights are now only on them. A country song plays in the background*.)*

Forgive me, but you look so familiar...

VICTORIO. Never saw you before in my life.

ANTHONY. Perfect, wasn't sure.

> *(**ANTHONY** sits next to him at the bar and tries to be as casual as possible expressing his interest but **VICTORIO** is too engaged in his drink and his phone.)*

Come here often?

VICTORIO. Nope.

ANTHONY. Did you hear the Spice Girls are forming a reunion tour?

---

* A license to produce MY BIG GAY ITALIAN CHRISTMAS does not include a performance license for any third-party or copyrighted music. Licensees should create an original composition or use music in the public domain. For further information, please see Music Use Note on page 3.

VICTORIO. Just when I thought you had used every possible pick up line.

ANTHONY. Who said I was trying to pick you up?

(**VICTORIO** *shoots him a look.*)

Okay, maybe I kind of was…

Honestly, I'm not from here and just looking to hang out.

VICTORIO. Same here. Victorio. Nice to meet you.

ANTHONY. Anthony, pleasure. Can I buy you a drink?

VICTORIO. I just got myself a double bourbon but thanks. So what brings you to Dallas?

ANTHONY. I own my own weight loss corporation and we have a huge location finally opening up in Texas.

VICTORIO. No way, which diet company??

ANTHONY. It's called "Body Body" …

VICTORIO. Get out!!! My Aunt Frances was on that and she lost two hundred pounds.

ANTHONY. No way! That's music to my ears.

VICTORIO. Well she said it was better than any other diet she ever went on and swears by it to all her friends.

ANTHONY. That's amazing. Tell her I will send her a free supply of "Body Body" Cannoli's just for that.

VICTORIO. Those are her favorite!

ANTHONY. Are you Italian?

VICTORIO. Victorio. Come on…what do you think?

ANTHONY. Good point.

VICTORIO. Off the boat! My mother was born in Sicily but I was born here.

ANTHONY. So, what do you do for work?

VICTORIO. I'm a heart surgeon.

ANTHONY. Get out! What brought you to Dallas?

VICTORIO. I'm overseeing a new hospital opening up in Waxahachie.

ANTHONY. Wow! Now THAT is impressive. I love Waxahachie! Beautiful this time of year actually, beautiful views...are you single?

VICTORIO. I was married to a woman once, but we broke apart as a couple and I finally found myself.

ANTHONY. Good for you. Kids?

VICTORIO. No kids.

ANTHONY. So...what's your type?

VICTORIO. Hmmm, I'm not sure...

Generally, a nice guys with eyes that tell me a story that can grab my attention. You?

(They lock eyes.)

ANTHONY. Italian heart surgeons who wear cowboy hats and have big green eyes.

VICTORIO. They're hazel.

ANTHONY. We were so close.

DJ. *(Voice over.)* Next up to the microphone we have Victorio!

ANTHONY. You sing karaoke?!

VICTORIO. Only when I'm drunk. Any requests?

ANTHONY. Surprise me.

VICTORIO. Perfect. Here you can wear my hat.

*(**VICTORIO** puts his hat on **ANTHONY**'s head.)*

ANTHONY. Are you crazy!? I can't wear this!

VICTORIO. It looks good on you.

> (**VICTORIO** *crosses center stage and takes the microphone as a spot light comes up on him and a light remains on* **ANTHONY**. **VICTORIO** *sings a beautiful solo that immediately registers with* **ANTHONY** *bringing back memories from his past. It begins very casual and then turns into* **VICTORIO** *making serious eye contact with* **ANTHONY** *during the song. Eventually* **VICTORIO** *will take* **ANTHONY**'s *hand and bring him to the stage and finish the song directly to him.* **VICTORIO** *touches his face and kissing him ever so gently at the conclusion of the song. As they kiss, the lights dissolve back up and they cross back as if mid-story.)*

It was right in that moment I knew Anthony was the one.

MARIA. That is the most adorable story. Oh my God I'm crying!

VICTORIO. Women become very emotional in their ninth month.

JOSEPHINE. Please, wait till you start menopause!

TONIANN. So, what happened after Dallas?

ANTHONY. Well we had such a great time in Dallas...

VICTORIO. So, I asked Anthony to join me in Vegas the following week.

ANTHONY. And we had such a great time there...

VICTORIO. So, I asked him to join me in Maui the following week.

ANTHONY. And we had such a great time in Maui...

VICTORIO. So, I asked him to join me in Paris the following week.

ANTHONY. And we had an incredible time everywhere we went. We are truly enjoying getting to know each other.

TONIANN. But I seriously must be doing something wrong! The furthest place a man ever took me is Atlantic City.

JOSEPHINE. Speaking of which, I'm going to the Golden Nugget for New Years if anyone wants to come with me.

ANGELA. You got a room on New Years!?

JOSEPHINE. My host Ralph D'Ambrosio is the best! Every time I call him he gives me whatever I need and then some!

TONIANN. *(To* **VICTORIO** *in a whisper.)* That's because she drops ten grand every time she goes there. She's a degenerate.

MARIA. Well I guess this would be a good time to give out my grab bag gift. I had you Cousin Josephine!

JOSEPHINE. I'm so happy! You always know what to get me.

(She opens the box to fifty dollars in chips.)

Fifty dollars in chips for the Golden Nugget! Maria you are the BEST! This is a great gift. Now I have all my gambling money for New Years Eve!!

TONIANN. *(To* **VICTORIO** *in a whisper.)* She is so full of shit. That will last her three minutes the way she gambles!

JOSEPHINE. Toniann, I had you in the grab bag. An easy one for me this year.

*(***JOSEPHINE*** *hands* **TONIANN** *an envelope.)*

TONIANN. How did I know you had me this year!? How did I know!?

  (**TONIANN** *opens to a fifty dollar Dunkin' Donuts gift card.*)

Dunkin' Donuts! How did you know Josephine!? My favorite!

I live on Dunkin' Donuts! Every morning without fail I go to Dunkin' Donuts. So thoughtful of you Josephine, Thank You!

JOSEPHINE. Do I know my Cousin? Or do I know my Cousin?

ANTHONY. Well I had Cousin Geraldine...

TONIANN. And I had Howie. Maria, did you call him?

MARIA. That's not necessary right now Aunt Toniann.

TONIANN. YES IT IS! I'm a nervous wreck with him on the roads like this.

MARIA. He won't drive if it's that bad.

ANGELA. Call his cell now and check on him please.

JOSEPHINE. No, what if he is driving? He can't text and drive or even talk and drive.

MARIA. We really don't need to call him.

ANGELA. We need to check on him, this is a nightmare! And what am I supposed to do leave the lasagna in the oven till New Years???

JOSEPHINE. I saw you have zucchini pasta in the fridge so you can just boil me a pot of water.

TONIANN. What if God forbid he's stuck!? Anthony call him on your phone.

MARIA. WE BROKE UP!!

We broke up. Howie and I have filed for divorce.

ANGELA. Oh my God, somebody get me a chair before I pass out!

(**ANTHONY** *gets her to a seat.*)

JOSEPHINE. Sweetie what happened?!

TONIANN. I never trusted that fuck! He left you nine months pregnant!

Is there another woman?

MARIA. NO, I left him. I couldn't take it any more. I just felt like he wasn't "the one," ya know…so I need to start over as soon as possible so I could find a compatible companion for the sake of my kids.

ANTHONY. So where is Howie really?

MARIA. He's home packing his stuff and watching Jonah. We agreed it would be too difficult to be together today.

JOSEPHINE. Oh my God, that poor man, packing to leave his own home on Christmas…

TONIANN. He's Jewish, he'll be fine.

Maria, you didn't want to wait till after the baby was born, it was that bad?

MARIA. It was horrible. I couldn't take it any more and I don't want to use this new baby as a band-aid for a wound that is too deep to ever be healed.

VICTORIO. Are you sure it's not your hormones Maria? They do run wild during pregnancy.

ANGELA. That's an excellent point Victorio! I threw a frying pan out the window at your father when I was pregnant with Peter. We used to fight like animals and look it all worked itself out. We were happy till the day he died.

MARIA. It's not the same Mom, I need to continue to pursue my acting and singing career and he wants me to be a stay at home Mom. I can't change for someone Mom, I can't!

ANGELA. So now you're going to pursue an acting career and a singing career while you have two kids running around with no husband!!?? Can someone please pinch me and wake me up today!?

TONIANN. Angela calm down, we will get past this and we will manage, we always do.

VICTORIO. If I may, I know this isn't my business but I think considering Maria's condition it would be best for her to not stress right now.

JOSEPHINE. He's right! Honey you need to relax, and Angela stop making this all about you. You always do that!

ANGELA. ME!!? I made a vegetable lasagna just for you and your fucking diet, who you kidding Josephine?

TONIANN. Ladies please! Ron Corning is talking!

NEWS ANCHOR. *(Voice over.)* We have just received word that President Trump has declared a complete State of Emergency for the entire tri-state area and has quadrupled the usual number of snow trucks for all effected areas. He just tweeted a statement "I will use all the funding necessary at this time to get everyone who is effected by this storm home safely." I have to say Carmela that it's great for American citizens who have twitter to see the President's statements so they have comfort at this time.

TONIANN. Thank God for Donald Trump! Thank God!!!

Remember that last storm we had when Obama was in office? My car was planted under three feet of snow for almost a month and he did NOTHING to help Staten Island, NOTHING!

VICTORIO. Well that's a little harsh don't you think Toniann?

TONIANN. No it's not harsh at all, look how he is helping the economy!?

And the traffic is much better now. Even when me and Baby Anna went to the mall, we were in and out in twenty minutes!

More people working, better incomes for families and less traffic.

Donald Trump is a saint!

   (**TONIANN** *stands up and raises her glass.*)

To making America great again!

VICTORIO. Will you excuse me for a second I think I need to use the men's room again.

   (**VICTORIO** *excuses himself for the men's room and* **ANTHONY** *rises animalistic when he is out of ear shot.*)

ANTHONY. How many times do I have to ask this family to NOT discuss politics on holidays! I can't believe you just embarrassed me Aunt Toniann!

TONIANN. What did I say!? Are you kidding me!?

Don't tell me he's a democrat?

ANTHONY. Yes he's a democrat! And he despises Trump! Why would you get into a conversation like that?

TONIANN. I didn't say anything, Carmine Lubriani said it!

ANTHONY. Oh please it's Fox News, Trump could murder all of 86th Street and they would say he didn't mean it.

TONIANN. Oh don't tell me you're becoming a democrat now too!?

JOSEPHINE. I heard most of the gays are...

ANGELA. I don't want to screw this up for Anthony, please let's table this conversation!

ANTHONY. Please for me can you just not go there and try I mean really try not to embarrass me...please! Change the subject.

(**VICTORIO** *returns.*)

JOSEPHINE. Oh Victorio, we were just discussing that your last name is so familiar to me, by any chance are you related to Frank Buccatini?

VICTORIO. I have a Cousin Frank but he lives in Biloxi now.

TONIANN. I love Canada! Gorgeous Country!

ANTHONY. Biloxi is in Mississippi Aunt Toniann.

TONIANN. Another gorgeous country!

ANTHONY. Mom, why don't Victorio and I go work on some stuff in the kitchen so you can sit with Maria and relax a little bit.

ANGELA. Since when do you help in the kitchen?

ANTHONY. Today.

(**ANTHONY** *takes* **VICTORIO** *and they exit off.*)

TONIANN. Was it something I said again?

ANGELA. Victorio is a doll! Maria we need to find you a nice Italian guy too!

JOSEPHINE. I don't know something is off with him, I can't put my finger on it yet...but I don't trust him.

ANGELA. Josephine you're like the kiss of death. How can you find something wrong with a successful, Italian, age appropriate, heart surgeon who reads books to his mother in a nursing home!

JOSEPHINE. I'm never wrong Angela! I'm telling you something is off!

(*A loud banging is heard at the door. Everyone is immediately startled.*)

Who the hell made it here in all this snow!

ANGELA. Josephine answer the door. Toniann hide Maria, it's probably that fucking Howie! Don't worry Maria I got this!

MARIA. MA! It's not Howie!

(*Banging continues.*)

JOSEPHINE. I got it! Calm your horses I'm coming!

(**JOSEPHINE** *answers to an animalistic* **OLIVIA. OLIVIA** *enters the house in a fur coat with her hair wind blown and sky high. She is trembling and wild and instantly puts everyone into "who the hell" is this mode.*)

OLIVIA. Merry Christmas! Now somebody better tell me who the FUCK is sleeping with my husband!

(*Everyone immediately looks to* **TONIANN.**)

TONIANN. Hold on! Hold on! Why is everyone looking at me! I had no idea he was married!

OLIVIA. You home-wrecker! Get over here you stupid bitch!

(**ANGELA** *and* **JOSEPHINE** *immediately run to grab her.*)

ANGELA. Seriously Toniann! Like I don't have enough stress on this holiday!

When are you going to stop sleeping with married men!

TONIANN. Lady I swear, Angela I swear! We went on three dates and he swore to me he was single!

OLIVIA. Where is he!? Where is he!?

TONIANN. He's in Brooklyn with his family.

OLIVIA. Liar! I followed him here and his car is outside!

TONIANN. What are you talking about!? I just spoke to Sal and he's in Brooklyn!

OLIVIA. SAL!!?? Is that the name he is going with that son of a bitch!

His name is Victorio you stupid slut!!

> *(***VICTORIO*** *and* ***ANTHONY*** *enter from the kitchen.* ***VICTORIO*** *locks eyes with* ***OLIVIA*** *and is stunned speechless. Everyone immediately realizes what is happening.)*

TONIANN. Okay, I'll let the stupid slut comment go.

ANTHONY. Victorio who is this woman?

TONIANN. Oh boy, Maybe we should excuse them.

JOSEPHINE. Are you crazy, sit down Toniann.

VICTORIO. Olivia I can explain.

ANTHONY. Who is she?

OLIVIA. I'm his wife!

Victorio I'm going to ask you this just once and you better be honest with me. Which one of these bitches are you sleeping with that you left me alone on CHRISTMAS DAY!

> *(Everyone is stunned and motionless till finally* ***ANTHONY*** *raises his hand.)*

What!!?? You're gay!! No this can't be, this can't be… I can't breathe… I can't breathe.

(**ANGELA**, **TONIANN** *and* **JOSEPHINE** *rush to her aide and take her coat off and get her to a seat and get her some water.*)

ANTHONY. Please tell me you're not married and this woman is crazy!

OLIVIA. Oh my God I'm going to throw up.

TONIANN. Anthony you didn't know?

ANTHONY. I had no idea, I'm just as shocked as she is right now!

How the hell could you be married!?

OLIVIA. This doesn't make any sense.

ANTHONY. This is a nightmare.

OLIVIA. It's just a bad dream right!?

(**VICTORIO** *rushes to her side.*)

VICTORIO. Please Olivia you have to understand that I've had feelings like this for years and I just didn't know what to do with them. I've been repressing all these emotions I've had for men for over two decades. I love you, I still love you but a year ago I started experimenting I discovered something about myself that I always knew but never could face. I didn't want to hurt you...

OLIVIA. So you decided to live a double life and never tell me any of this!?

Is that how you didn't want to hurt me Victorio?! Seriously!

JOSEPHINE. Ya know Oprah did a special on this once!?

ANTHONY. Olivia, I'm so sorry I had no idea.

Victorio get the fuck out of my house.

VICTORIO. I can't leave Olivia like this.

ANTHONY. She can stay.

VICTORIO. Anthony! I love you! You know that! Do you think I would sacrifice so much if I didn't!?

ANTHONY. When we were in Paris you told me a whole story about how you left your wife two years ago and last year you re-connected with some guy who was gay that you met in medical school. NOW, I find out you have a wife all this time. I don't believe anything that comes out of your mouth!

OLIVIA. Paris!!? You took him to Paris!!??

JOSEPHINE. Get her a martini Toniann

OLIVIA. Get me the bottle!!

TONIANN. Well think of it this way Olivia, wouldn't you rather he cheated on you with a guy rather than another woman.

OLIVIA. I think another woman would have been a little easier!

TONIANN. See now I completely disagree, I mean when a man leaves me for another man than there is nothing I can do about that. When a guy leaves me for another woman I want to rip his face off and her face off.

(**OLIVIA** *collects herself and rises to* **VICTORIO.**)

OLIVIA. Victorio, I have never been so disappointed in anyone as I am in you right now. You spent twenty years of marriage in a lie! Not only did you lie to yourself but you lied to me. You ruined my life Victorio. I will never ever forgive you for this!

Ever! I am going home and I am packing my things and I can promise you, you will never see me again. Have an amazing gay fucking life.

(**OLIVIA** *begins to exit and walks smack in to* **OFFICER KELLY GARDNER** *who has just entered herself in the house.*)

KELLY. HOLD IT RIGHT THERE LADY!

OLIVIA. Merry Fucking Christmas excuse me!

KELLY. We have a problem!

Everyone stay right where you are and no one move!

No one is going anywhere tonight!

OLIVIA. Bullshit lady! I'm out of here.

KELLY. ARE YOU OUT OF YOUR FUCKING MIND! You go nowhere!

Now listen up! I'm Sergeant Kelly Gardner of the one twenty two Precinct and we have just received word from transit authorities and the mayor's office that we are under a State of Emergency. All the roads are shut down. NO ONE LEAVES THIS HOUSE!

JOSEPHINE. Oh my God!

OLIVIA. I couldn't care less Officer. I have to leave this house!

VICTORIO. Olivia you can't risk your life in the state you are in!

JOSEPHINE. Plus she had half a bottle of vodka!!!

KELLY. I will pretend I didn't hear that! Miss you need to stay right where you are. I know the holidays sometimes bring out some emotions...

OLIVIA. Emotions!? I just found out that my husband is a homosexual and he's been having an affair with HIM for six months and while I'm home trying to figure out how to improve our sex life, he's with Anthony in Paris drinking champagne under the Eiffel fucking Tower!

KELLY. Okay that's pretty harsh. Wow! Well I'm sorry you're having a terrible holiday but you still need to stay here in the house.

Everyone needs to stay put. Now if you will excuse me I have to alert the rest of the neighborhood.

OLIVIA. Officer please take me with you!

KELLY. That is a very tempting offer but you are going to just have to stay here and relax. Merry Christmas everyone!

(**OFFICER GARDNER** *exits.*)

VICTORIO. Olivia, please can you just calm down and relax maybe we can go talk somewhere in private.

ANGELA. I think that's a wonderful idea. Why don't you guys go in the guest bedroom.

(**OLIVIA** *hesitates but* **VICTORIO** *makes a pleading gesture and she finally agrees and they walk off stage.*)

JOSEPHINE. Anthony, how are you holding up with all this?

ANTHONY. Well you know the saying, "If it looks too good to be true..."

TONIANN. You can't think like that Anthony.

MARIA. You seriously have no luck with men do you?

ANGELA. EHEM! I don't think you should talk Maria!

TONIANN. He gets it from me, I'm telling you this family is cursed when it comes to men. Anthony clearly can't catch a break lately, Maria is nine months pregnant and going through a divorce, I've had five husbands and five divorces, Angela your husband dropped dead and Josephine...well what's your story are you a lesbian?

JOSEPHINE. *(She hesitates.)* Yes...

ANGELA. WHAT!!

TONIANN. Finally! Twenty years later she finally comes out!

MARIA. Since when? I had no idea!

ANGELA. I'm stunned speechless!

TONIANN. Oh please you can't see she's a lesbian!

ANTHONY. Helen Keller can see she's a lesbian.

JOSEPHINE. You're not exactly Arnold Schwarzenegger Anthony!

ANGELA. Are you seeing anyone Josephine?

TONIANN. Donna Annobile am I right?

JOSEPHINE. How did you know?

TONIANN. You were living with her for ten years!

JOSEPHINE. Well we broke up! She left me for Patti Testaverde can you believe it? I've been single a few years.

TONIANN. WOW! This family really is cursed!

> *(A group of nuns are heard outside singing Christmas Carols.* **ANTHONY** *runs to the window.)*

ANTHONY. Oh look the nuns are singing in the snow storm.

TONIANN. They sound amazing.

ANGELA. Thank God for them, I was beginning to forget it was Christmas.

MARIA. They must be freezing out there.

> *(A knock is heard at the door and* **ANTHONY** *opens it to* **SISTER FABIANA** *and* **SISTER FONZINA.***)*

FONZINA. BUON NATALE!

FABIANA. I'm freezing my ass off!

TONIANN. Merry Christmas Sisters!!!

ANGELA. You must be freezing!

FABIANA. We are okay my child!

FONZINA. Please excuse us. I'm Sister Fonzina and this is my sister, Sister Fabiana. We tried so hard to sing our prayers through the storm but God had a different plan for us this evening with this horrible blizzard.

FABIANA. It's too cold. We had to take a break!

ANGELA. Of course! Of course! Please make yourself at home. Are you hungry? Can I get you anything?

FONZINA. No please we are fine, we didn't come to impose.

TONIANN. Can you believe this storm ladies, they said we are getting almost three feet of snow!

FABIANA. Our lord wanted us to remember his birthday today, I believe he is sending a VERY powerful message.

ANTHONY. You could say that again!

JOSEPHINE. What's the message?

FONZINA. If we pray and listen his message will come.

> (**FONZINA** *and* **FABIANA** *kneel downstage and begin to pray. They pray quietly in Italian when after a few moments* **OLIVIA** *is heard screaming off stage.*)

OLIVIA. Twenty years I gave you! Twenty years you took from me you selfish, heartless, motherfucker!

> (*The nuns look up stunned and everyone looks to* **ANTHONY.**)

ANTHONY. It's the Real Housewives of New Jersey Marathon on Bravo.

(**OLIVIA** *comes storming out with* **VICTORIO.**)

OLIVIA. I need a fucking drink!

Oh sisters I'm so sorry!! I didn't know there were more people here I thought the roads were still closed.

FABIANA. It was too cold to sing so we came in for a quick break.

ANGELA. Are you guys working things out?

OLIVIA. Working things out? I want to cut his balls off Angela!

FONZINA. My child, you speak with such hatred! What has he done?

OLIVIA. Go ahead tell them Victorio. Confess your sins!

ANTHONY. This is all my fault!

OLIVIA. No Anthony, it's not your fault my husband is gay.

ANGELA. No one is to blame in this but society! Society still has people scared to come out and that's why Josephine never told anyone she was a lesbian and Victorio never told anyone he was gay!

OLIVIA. I don't care that he's gay, I care that he married me and stayed with me for twenty years.

FONZINA. We should probably go...

FABIANA. Are you crazy!? This is good, shut up and sit down.

ANGELA. Oh My God!! Breaking news again!! Toniann make Ron Corning louder!

(**TONIANN** *grabs the remote and makes the television louder as everyone watches the news.*)

NEWS ANCHOR. *(Voice over.)* The National Weather Society is calling this the WORST storm in New York history!!

MARIA. Ughhhh!

NEWS ANCHOR. *(Voice over.)* Over five thousand flights are cancelled now across the tri-state area and all major airports from DC all the way up to Bangor are closed!

MARIA. OH NO! OH MY GOD!

NEWS ANCHOR. *(Voice over.)* By the end of the night we are expecting anywhere from three to five million power outages!

MARIA. AHHHHHHHH!!!

NEWS ANCHOR. *(Voice over.)* People could be stranded without power for days!!

MARIA. AHHHHHH!!!!!!!

    (MARIA now is screaming for dear life.)

ANGELA. Maria what the hell is the matter with you!? I have plenty of food, candles and a backup generator!

MARIA. My water broke!

    (Black out.)

End Act One

ACT TWO

*(Direct pick up of everyone in the same positions. Lights up on **MARIA** screaming…)*

ANGELA. WHAT!!??

MARIA. My water broke!

(Everyone ad libs in panic.)

FONZINA. Sweet Jesus!

TONIANN. Saint Anthony!!

FABIANA. CALL THE DOCTOR!!

VICTORIO. I'm a Doctor. Everyone calm down!

ANGELA. You're a heart surgeon!?

VICTORIO. Yes, which makes me even more qualified to examine your daughter. Maria let's get you to the bedroom so I can examine you.

ANTHONY. Don't you even think about touching my sister's vagina you son of a bitch! Toniann call an ambulance.

TONIANN. Fine, what's the number?

ALL. 911

> *(**TONIANN** works feverishly on her phone as others try their phones.)*

TONIANN. No service!

ANGELA. What difference does it make!? They will never get through the storm.

MARIA. AHHHHHHH!!

(**MARIA** *whales and crouches in pain.*)

VICTORIO. Maria relax you're in good hands, go lay on the bed I will be right there. I need you to relax.

(**MARIA** *exits screaming.*)

I know you hate me right now Anthony and you have every right to, but your sister is in danger and I can help her so please if you can just find it in you...

OLIVIA. He's right. Let him go Anthony. He may be a lying piece of shit but he's still one of the best doctors in the country.

ANGELA. Anthony please...

ANTHONY. GO!

FABIANA. We can help we are nurses!

FONZINA. Yes! Please let us help, the good Lord sent us here for a reason!

VICTORIO. Are you really qualified nurses?

FONZINA. Yes we got our degrees in Sicily!

FABIANA. Well I dropped out to become a prostitute but I know what I'm doing!

FONZINA. Fabiana!!!

VICTORIO. Works for me! Wash up ladies, we have a baby to deliver!

(**VICTORIO** *exits.*)

JOSEPHINE. Wait I just started boiling water on the stove go grab it!

ANGELA. No I put olive oil in it you ass!

FABIANA. NO!! That's good for the baby! She will slide out nice!

FONZINA. I'll go get it!

(They scramble to exit.)

ANGELA. My nerves are shot! I need a xanax!

JOSEPHINE. I'd be on the floor dying of heart attack right now if I were you Angela, I don't know how you do it!

ANGELA. That's very comforting Josephine thank you!

OLIVIA. Well if this isn't crazy circumstances, I don't know what is…

TONIANN. Do you need a drink sweetie? This must be a lot for you.

OLIVIA. You have no idea.

*(***OLIVIA*** sits. ***ANTHONY*** grabs a drink and sits beside her.)*

ANTHONY. Drink this it will make you feel better.

OLIVIA. I don't blame you Anthony, I don't.

ANTHONY. Thank you. I honestly had no idea you existed. I never would have let this go on the way it did if I knew.

OLIVIA. It's not your fault.

JOSEPHINE. It's more common than you know Olivia, trust me I know.

OLIVIA. Do you know how many gay friends I have!?

Trust me I know! I just didn't ever think it would effect my life.

ANGELA. Well at least you never had kids.

OLIVIA. I wanted kids.

ANTHONY. You did? Why didn't you have them?

OLIVIA. Victorio can't…create kids. We did everything we possibly could and finally gave up after way too many false hopes. So not only did I sacrifice twenty years of marriage but I gave up any chance I ever had of having children.

> (**TONIANN** *takes her cue and pours more vodka in her glass.*)

TONIANN. You're gonna need some more babe.

JOSEPHINE. Well look at it this way Olivia, at least you know now!

OLIVIA. And what good does it do me now!? I'm forty-five years old, I can't have kids.

JOSEPHINE. Sure you can!! That's not too old!

Do you still have…

> (*She tries to be discreet for* **ANTHONY**'s *benefit.*)

your friend?

ANTHONY. Oh please Josephine!

OLIVIA. Yeah, but what am I going to do now!

The point is I loved Victorio and I made a life with him.

I never had kids because of him.

JOSEPHINE. Well anything can happen Olivia, my Nonna had ten kids and she was fifty-five when she gave birth to Aunt Lou Lou.

ANGELA. No she wasn't!

TONIANN. She was forty-five Josephine!

JOSEPHINE. NO! She was a change of life baby! Don't you remember the doctors thought she was a tumor 'till the seventh month!

TONIANN. You're so full of shit Josephine that's not what happened!

She re-writes history my cousin!

ANGELA. She wasn't fifty-five Josephine.

JOSEPHINE. You all have select memory! Besides I was the closest to Nonna so I remember all the stories detail for detail.

TONIANN. Now she was the closest to Nonna!

ANGELA. Well she kind of was Toniann I'll give her that.

JOSEPHINE. I used to help her cook every Sunday! She taught me how to make homemade cavatelli when I was five!

TONIANN. I helped her every Sunday too Josephine!

ANGELA. Oh please who you kidding Toniann!?

TONIANN. I did!

ANGELA. You were out partying 'till four in the morning every night!

No one ever saw you on Sunday's!

JOSEPHINE. That's right! Who the hell saw you!?

TONIANN. Well at least I had a life!? What can I say I was popular.

JOSEPHINE. *(Coughs.)* Boutanna!!

ANGELA. Do they have this in your family too Olivia?

OLIVIA. Oh of course they do!

ANGELA. So you're Italian?

OLIVIA. Full blooded, my maiden name is Tuttarosa.

TONIANN. Olivia Tuttarosa! I love it, like the tomatoes!

OLIVIA. The best tomatoes on the market!

ANGELA. I disagree, but my son is sleeping with your husband so I won't argue about tomatoes.

OLIVIA. It's all good Angela. I'm honestly very sorry about barging in like this. You seem like a really nice family.

TONIANN. It's no bother Olivia, I would of barged in just as crazy as you did.

*(**FONZINA** enters.)*

FONZINA. Maria is six centimeters dilated

ANGELA. Oh my god the baby is coming!

JOSEPHINE. Does this mean she is in actual labor Angela?

ANTHONY. Even I know that's what that means!

ANGELA. What can we do sister!?

FONZINA. I need you all to stay calm and just try and relax. Doctor Buccatini is doing an incredible job. Fabiana is preparing the water and making Maria some cold compresses.

Everyone just stay put and try to keep busy and pray to Saint Anthony!

*(**FONZINA** goes back in the bedroom.)*

ANGELA. Oh my God, I'm a wreck.

ANTHONY. Mom, calm down! Everything will be fine. You heard her.

JOSEPHINE. Your mother and my mother and all our aunts and uncles were born in the house and they all turned out fine.

TONIANN. No they were not you ass! My mother was born in a hospital and so was yours.

JOSEPHINE. Don't tell me Toniann! I know where my mother was born!

TONIANN. I'm telling you she makes up stories!

ANGELA. Aunt Mary was born in the house and the rest were born in hospitals where I would feel much more safe if that's where my daughter was right now!

OLIVIA. She really is in the best hands Angela, my husband may be a lying, cheating, gay fuck but he is the best doctor in the country.

ANGELA. Thank You Olivia, that really helps.

Are you okay? Can I get you anything?

OLIVIA. I'm okay, I'm just asking myself...what comes next?

I mean I thought I had everything figured out and now this.

I just feel blindsided and totally fucking lost right now.

TONIANN. I know exactly what you are going through Olivia!

JOSEPHINE. Of course she does.

TONIANN. No, seriously...when my fourth husband Vito left me, I was absolutely devastated! I was your age at the time and I thought my life was over!

OLIVIA. He left you for a man?

TONIANN. No he left me for a twenty-five year old flight attendant! While I was home doing his laundry and working out at the gym to make sure my ass and my love handles never got too big, he was flying the friendly skies every week with Claudette! To this day I can't get on a plane without having an emotional breakdown.

ANTHONY. I don't think that's the best story to help Olivia, Toniann.

JOSEPHINE. I agree, not at all Anthony. I know exactly what Olivia needs.

A tarot card reading!!!

ANTHONY. Oh Jesus. Here we go!

(*JOSEPHINE jumps up to get her purse which has the tarot cards inside and pulls them out. They are wrapped in old fashioned tin foil.*)

JOSEPHINE. Whenever shit like this happens I pull out the cards and we can see exactly where you are supposed to be headed.

TONIANN. She thinks she is Miss Fucking Cleo my cousin.

JOSEPHINE. I have the gift and you know it Toniann.

TONIANN. Yeah the gift of bullshit!

JOSEPHINE. My Nonna always told me that I had the gift just like her.

Remember Angela??!

ANGELA. Nanny did have a sixth sense, I will say that for sure.

JOSEPHINE. And she always said baby Josephine has it too because I used to say things as a kid and they would happen.

I can't control it! So when she died she left me these in her will.

TONIANN. She did not leave you those in the will, you went through all her shit and took all her stuff.

JOSEPHINE. She wanted me to have these Toniann, don't tell me!!!

TONIANN. And she wanted you to have her wedding band also, and all her China right!?

JOSEPHINE. Of course she did! It was in the will!

ANGELA. How come I never saw this will?!

TONIANN. I want to see Nonna's will!

JOSEPHINE. It's buried somewhere now can we focus on Olivia please.

All this bad energy pollutes the room and we can't get a read. Now Olivia take the cards and shuffle. Anthony get me the olive oil.

> (**ANTHONY** *goes and gets olive oil while* **OLIVIA** *shuffles the cards.*)

Now I'm going to put a drop of this olive oil on my hands and Anthony come here, you go first since you are part of Olivia's new fate.

> (**JOSEPHINE** *puts the olive oil on* **ANTHONY**'s *finger and on her own finger.*)

Now Anthony flip the first card.

ANTHONY. How old are these cards Josephine?

JOSEPHINE. Your great-grandmother got them from her great-grandmother in Sicily many centuries ago.

TONIANN. Yeah of course she did, and Mary Magdalene got them from her grandmother who got them to the three wise men who got them from Moses. Josephine you are so full of shit with these stories!

> (**ANTHONY** *flips the card.*)

ALL. Ohhhhhhhhh...

JOSEPHINE. Look at that Anthony, you are the Queen!!!

ANTHONY. I didn't need the psychic friends network to tell me that Josephine.

JOSEPHINE. But look, not only you are the Queen but read, you are the Queen of...

ANTHONY. Testicles?

JOSEPHINE. NO you ass! Pentacles! You are the Queen of Pentacles!

TONIANN. Congrats! Have a rice ball!

ANTHONY. So what does that mean Josephine?

JOSEPHINE. It means that you are in charge of your destiny and the future you seek will be given to you at the palm of the universe.

ANTHONY/ OLIVIA / TONIANN. Thank God!!

JOSEPHINE. Now Olivia your turn.

(JOSEPHINE *puts some of the olive oil on* OLIVIA*'s hands and she turns a card over. Everyone comes and looks and is immediately horrified.)*

OLIVIA. Oh my God the death card!!!

SEE! I told you I had bad luck! My husband's gay and I'm gonna die! Merry Christmas!!

JOSEPHINE. That's not what the death card means Olivia, it could mean all kinds of things.

OLIVIA. Like what?!

(MARIA *is heard off stage whaling in pain.)*

JOSEPHINE. It could mean a birth!

ANGELA. Oh my God my poor baby! She needs an epidural!!

TONIANN. Alright I'll go tell him!

ANTHONY. I'm sure he knows that Toniann, He didn't think to pack one in the car.

ANGELA. I need to be in there!

(*Nuns re-enter.)*

FONZINA. She is eight centimeters dilated! She has started crowning.

I think we can see a head!

FABIANA. Jesus is here! This a Christmas birth of faith and hope!

FONZINA. Oh stop being so dramatic!

ANGELA. Oh my God! I need to be in there!

FONZINA. NO! You have to stay here! We are not in a sterile environment and we need to reduce the risk of infection.

ANGELA. So how are all of you sterile?

FONZINA. From the snow. I told you, God had a plan for us. Now please stay calm and just pray.

(They exit.)

OLIVIA. Angela, seriously she is in good hands.

ANGELA. Thank you, I just seriously can't take this right now.

It's too much!

TONIANN. Maybe we should all sit nice and have the lasagna while Maria gives birth.

ANGELA. Are you serious Toniann?

TONIANN. Well what are we supposed to do, starve while she gives birth?

ANGELA. Olivia are you hungry?

OLIVIA. Don't worry about me! I found my date for this Christmas.

*(**OLIVIA** holds up the bottle of vodka and pours the rest.)*

TONIANN. Best date I ever had!

OLIVIA. Cheers to that!

So Anthony, I have to ask...and please don't take it personal but are you having sex with my husband?

ANTHONY. Oh my God!

JOSEPHINE. Did she just ask him that?

ANGELA. On second thought let me go check on the lasagna and get the Antipasto!

(**ANGELA** *exits.*)

OLIVIA. I'm sorry but I have to know. Because I'm not having sex with my husband so I need to know for my own sanity that someone is.

ANTHONY. I'm having sex with your husband.

TONIANN. Oh my God!

JOSEPHINE. Anthony you didn't!?

ANTHONY. What do you think gay men do!? Play mah-jongg!

TONIANN. But you don't tell his wife that!

ANTHONY. She asked!

OLIVIA. No seriously I needed to know that! It actually makes me feel better!

ANTHONY. Really!?

OLIVIA. Toniann was right! You have something that I can't give him.

I spent years thinking it was me and trying to fix myself so I can please him.

JOSEPHINE. You're gorgeous stop! Are you kidding!? Every lesbian in America would go nuts over you!!

OLIVIA. Maybe that's what I should do! Cause men suck!

JOSEPHINE. Maybe that's what the death card was telling you Olivia!

TONIANN. Don't listen to her! She's an idiot! Seriously Josephine!

OLIVIA. I wish I was a lesbian, but I like men too much.

(**ANGELA** *re-enters with antipasto tray.*)

So Anthony one more question and I swear I won't ask any more. Who is doing who?

JOSEPHINE. She wants to know whose the top? I can't take it!

ANGELA. Would you look at that there is not enough mozzarella on my antipasto tray, I'll be right back.

OLIVIA. You really don't have to answer that, I'm sorry the vodka is going to my head. I don't really want to know.

JOSEPHINE. Well shit, now I want to know!

ANTHONY. Well, I mean it's not always that simple to explain anyway.

TONIANN. How do you guys decide that?

ANTHONY. We flip a coin Toniann. I don't know it just happens!

TONIANN. But you always said you were the top Anthony, is that not the case with Victorio?

(**ANTHONY** *tries to mouth to* **TONIANN** *to shut up but it's too late and* **ANTHONY** *cringes.*)

OLIVIA. Oh my GOD! My husband is a bottom, I seriously can't take this right now!

TONIANN. Are you crazy that should make you feel so much better! Now you know that Anthony has something that only a boy can give him!

(**ANGELA** *re-enters.*)

ANGELA. Change the subject right now and eat my antipasto!

(**MARIA** *whales in pain again.*)

I can't take this, I can't take this.

TONIANN. Calm down Angela!

(*Nuns re-enter.*)

FONZINA. I need everyone to stay calm but we are having some complications.

ANGELA. What complications?

FONZINA. The baby and the cord are not in the best position.

So Doctor Buccatini is working feverishly to get a handle on it.

ANGELA. Oh my God! What can we do? What am I supposed to do?

FABIANA. Pray! Scream and cry and pray to every saint that is awake and can hear you!

FONZINA. That's what you tell her Fabiana!? Seriously???

(*They exit.*)

ANGELA. I'm certainly not going to stand here and pray while my daughter is in distress.

(**ANGELA** *exits off stage to where the front door is established and screams.*)

Officer Help!! Please EMERGENCY!! Somebody help!!

Officer!!

JOSEPHINE. Angela calm down.

ANTHONY. Let me try 911 again.

TONIANN. Angela you need to calm down!

ANTHONY. Damn no service!

ANGELA. Officer!!!

(**OFFICER GARDNER** *re-enters.*)

KELLY. What's the matter?

ANGELA. My daughter is in labor.

OLIVIA. My ex-husband is a doctor and delivering the baby in the guestroom.

JOSEPHINE. But the nun said there are major complications and they are both in horrible danger!

TONIANN. This is not the time to exaggerate Josephine!

KELLY. Everyone stay calm! Your husband is a doctor?

OLIVIA. One of the top heart surgeons in the country.

KELLY. She is in way better hands than she would be if she was at Staten Island Hospital! We just sent over forty people there with injuries and they have a skeleton crew with two doctors still in residency.

OLIVIA. She is in hard labor Angela, she can't go anywhere like that.

KELLY. I will do what I can but I'm sure I don't need to tell you how bad the roads are on this island.

TONIANN. You're telling me! That's cause there are way too many people on Staten Island!

KELLY. Well thank God for Donald Trump! We are all going to see even more improvements if they just leave him right where he is!

TONIANN. Exactly! That's what I've been saying! This fucking doctor in there is a die hard Democrat!

KELLY. Shit! Say no more, I'll see what I can do!

> (**KELLY** *exits.* **ANTHONY** *and* **OLIVIA** *pull* **ANGELA** *down on the couch.*)

OLIVIA. Everything is going to be fine Angela. Trust me.

ANGELA. Thank You Olivia. I know this is a horrible time for you. For both of you.

ANTHONY. The only thing I think we all care about right now is that Maria and that baby are okay.

ANGELA. How could I let this happen! I'm so pissed at myself!

ANTHONY. What could you have done Ma!

ANGELA. Told my daughter to stay home or took her to a hospital before the storm started.

ANTHONY. She wasn't even in labor, this is just a fluke.

OLIVIA. Anthony is right. And you heard Officer Gardner, if she was in the hospital she would be in the hands of God knows who!

ANTHONY. Victorio is an excellent surgeon!

OLIVIA. One of the best in the country, you can just ask him yourself.

Trust me he could be very cocky about it!

ANTHONY. You're telling me, he always has to let you know he knows more than everyone else.

OLIVIA. Right or wrong!! When we were in New Hope last summer he got into a huge argument with another doctor we are friends with over something so ridiculous just to prove he knew more than he did.

ANTHONY. I know! He did the same thing to me in Saint Barts! We were on the beach and we met this nice gay couple and they were BOTH doctors. Well of course Victorio had to prove he was the best.

OLIVIA. I'm going overnight to New Hope and you're going to Saint Barts. Toniann!!!

TONIANN. I gotcha sister!

(**TONIANN** *refills her glass.*)

OLIVIA. Eden Rock Hotel!?

ANTHONY. Hotel Christopher Saint Barth, with the two infinity pools.

OLIVIA. That fuck! I was dying to go there!

ANTHONY. I'll take you.

OLIVIA. Not your fault Anthony, not your fault at all.

TONIANN. Is it me or does Olivia feel like family?

JOSEPHINE. I'm doing Easter Olivia, you're welcome to come!

ANGELA. Good I'll start putting my requests in now. Farm to table diet you pain in the ass.

OLIVIA. Doesn't work! Tried it!

TONIANN. Thank you!

OLIVIA. Do "Body Body" it's the best diet plan on the market.

*(Everyone looks at **ANTHONY** stunned.)*

TONIANN. Were you on that plan Olivia?

OLIVIA. Yes I was! Lost fifty pounds!!

TONIANN. Well my nephew happens to be the owner and founder of "Body Body" Incorporated!

OLIVIA. Shut!

Up!

ANTHONY. I am.

OLIVIA. The "Body Body" cannoli's are to die for!! Are you serious right now!?

ANTHONY. I will see to it that you have a lifetime supply.

JOSEPHINE. It's the least you can do if your banging her husband.

ANGELA. Really Josephine!

> (*MARIA whales again. This time much louder.*)

I'm gonna pass out!

> (**TONIANN** *and* **ANGELA** *get her to a chair.*)

TONIANN. Josephine get her a xanax!

ANGELA. I already took five!

ANTHONY. Mom, calm down. I'm sure that's normal, isn't it!?

> (**MARIA** *screams again even louder.*)

ANGELA. No it's not normal, they have drugs for this now.

TONIANN. But they didn't use to and we all survived.

JOSEPHINE. She's fine Angela.

ANGELA. How the hell would you two know! You never had kids!

You have no idea what she is going through. Oh My God what if she needs an emergency c-section!

TONIANN. Don't even go there Angela!

ANGELA. Anthony was an emergency c-section! I spent forty-eight hours in fucking labor before they figured it out.

TONIANN. And see he came out fine!

ANGELA. I was in a hospital Toniann! I needed four blood transfusions!

Oh my God what if it's genetic!? What if Maria needs that!?

ANTHONY. Mom, calm down! If she had that problem she would have had it with Jonah.

JOSEPHINE. Exactly! She's a warrior! Just like me! She's a Bianco all the way!

TONIANN. She is definitely a Bianco!

JOSEPHINE. And what did Nonna always say about the Bianco's?

TONIANN / JOSEPHINE / ANGELA. Bianco's are fighters not feelers!

OLIVIA. Wait who is Bianco?

JOSEPHINE. Well our grandmother was a Bianco. My mother and Angela and Toniann's mother are sisters. They are Naso and my Mom married Joseph Marco so I'm Josephine Marco.

OLIVIA. That's so random because my grandfather was Fortunato Bianco.

TONIANN. Very common name Bianco.

JOSEPHINE. Wait a second. Our great-uncle is Fortunato Bianco.

TONIANN. Here we go with the stories.

ANGELA. No she's right! One of the brothers from eighteenth Avenue in Brooklyn was Fortunato!

JOSEPHINE. That's Florence and Anna's father!

OLIVIA. Oh my God! Now I really need to sit down.

ANTHONY. I think I may need to sit down.

OLIVIA. Florence and Anna are my Aunts! My fathers two sisters!

TONIANN. Shut up!!!

ANGELA. We haven't spoken to that side of the family in ages.

JOSEPHINE. I remember the whole story!

TONIANN. Of course you do Josephine!

JOSEPHINE. Don't you remember!? Nonna stopped talking to half her siblings when her father died because all hell broke loose at the wake!

TONIANN. That actually sounds familiar Josephine.

ANGELA. No she's right! The goumada showed up in the funeral home and Aunt Regina kicked her out!

JOSEPHINE. Uncle Tony got pissed and caused a whole boudelle in the funeral home.

TONIANN. And we know how they all carried grudges.

JOSEPHINE. I guess that's where you get it from Toniann.

TONIANN. Shut the fuck up Josephine.

ANGELA. So wait, if our great Uncle Fortunato is your grandfather.

Then makes us all...

JOSEPHINE. COUSINS!!!

ANTHONY. Oh my God... I'm banging my cousin's husband!

> *(They all scream and hug and kiss and laugh.* **OLIVIA** *falls on the couch from laughing so hard. While they are all ad-libbing and carrying on a subtle cry from off-stage is heard and they all stop and listen.* **ANGELA** *gets immediately choked up and they all comfort her in suspense when the nuns come out with the baby.)*

FABIANA. Merry Christmas!

FONZINA. It's a beautiful baby girl.

> *(They all go over.)*

ANGELA. Oh my God! Oh my God!

Does she have all ten fingers and ten toes.

FONZINA. Yes she does! Doctor Buccatini says she is a true blessing!

The Lord was with us today!

FABIANA. A Christmas miracle!

TONIANN. She's gorgeous!!

ANTHONY. She looks like me!

ANGELA. She does look like you! Definitely an Italian baby!

FONZINA. Italian all the way!

FABIANA. Come on Nonna let's go clean the bambina!

>   (**FONZINA** *hands the baby to* **ANGELA** *and they walk off stage.*)

FONZINA. I didn't want to tell anyone but that baby truly is a miracle.

Thank the good Lord for Doctor Buccatini!

ANTHONY. Well at least he did something right.

FONZINA. No, Anthony you don't understand, the cord was wrapped around the baby's neck bad. We almost lost her but Doctor Buccatini handled it perfectly and saved her life.

OLIVIA. He really is the best at what he does, he is.

FONZINA. The man is a saint!

ANTHONY / OLIVIA. Don't get carried away!

>   (**VICTORIO** *comes out. Everyone is speechless for a moment.*)

VICTORIO. Mother and child will be just fine.

TONIANN. Well on behalf of the family, thank you very much Victorio. We heard it wasn't easy.

VICTORIO. Eh, nothing a trained physician can't handle.

ANTHONY. Thank You Victorio.

VICTORIO. Thank you for trusting me.

So, is everything okay out here?

OLIVIA. Anthony's family has been amazing. Truly.

JOSEPHINE. Well you are family Olivia!

TONIANN. Mouth! Shut up!

VICTORIO. Did I miss something?

ANTHONY. Olivia is my third cousin twice removed.

JOSEPHINE. Second cousin three times removed.

TONIANN. No she's our second cousin, Anthony's third cousin!

VICTORIO. I need to sit down.

JOSEPHINE. Small fucking world right Victorio!

VICTORIO. Well I'm glad everyone got to know each other.

> (**MARIA** *comes out limping and* **JOSEPHINE,** **VICTORIO** *and* **TONIANN** *immediately rush to her aid and bring her to the couch.*)

TONIANN. What are you doing out of bed Maria?

MARIA. I need to see my daughter.

JOSEPHINE. Mom has her, they are cleaning her up now.

FONZINA. She's perfect Maria! A blessing from heaven this baby!

MARIA. I owe you my life Victorio.

VICTORIO. You owe me nothing Maria.

> (**FONZINA** *and* **ANGELA** *come out with the baby.* **ANGELA** *is holding her and brings her*

to **MARIA** *on the couch as everyone looks at her and makes sweet reactions.)*

ANGELA. Maria, she is so gorgeous! I am so proud of you baby!

JOSEPHINE. She's a fighter! Who needs an epidural? Right Maria!?

MARIA. I'm just happy these xanax are kicking in right now.

VICTORIO. I told you, much quicker under the tongue.

ANGELA. Anthony go get my bag I have to try that!

ANTHONY. Stop! Everyone is fine. What are you going to name her Maria?

MARIA. I found the perfect name for her during labor. She's a Pasqualina.

ALL. Awwwww... Pasqualina...

ANGELA. Where did you come up with Pasqualina?!

MARIA. Well on Easter we say Buona Pasqua! And since the baby was born the same day as Jesus and she's a miracle she has to be a Pasqualina.

FABIANA. Gorgeous! Gorgeous! Gorgeous!!

FONZINA. A blessing she is for sure! I think it's beautiful.

TONIANN. A miracle and a blessing!

MARIA. And her middle name is Victoria. After the beautiful doctor who saved her life. I will never be able to thank you enough Victorio.

VICTORIO. You don't have to Maria. I'm honored.

JOSEPHINE. Pasqualina Victoria! What a GORGEOUS name!

ANTHONY. Are you all high it sucks! Pasqualina Victoria Horowitz!?

What are her friends gonna call her? What are we gonna call her?

MARIA. Baby Pasqua!

TONIANN. Awwww...little pasqua.

JOSEPHINE. I love it!

MARIA. And this baby is a Pinnunziato!

She will be Pasqualina Victoria Pinnunziato!

TONIANN. Much better!

JOSEPHINE. Much!!

ANTHONY. Pasqualina Pinnunziato!? She sounds like a pasta dish!

ANGELA. Maria, how is Howie going to handle his daughter not having his last name?

MARIA. Easily. Howie isn't the father.

(Everyone is in shock.)

ANGELA. What do you mean Howie isn't the father!?

MARIA. I think the xanax are going to my head Doctor Buccatini!

ANGELA. Maria, if Howie isn't the baby's father...who is?

MARIA. Nino!

ANGELA. Who the fuck is Nino!?

JOSEPHINE. He sounds Italian!

ANGELA. Maria who is Nino!?

MARIA. Nino Fallacci!

ANGELA. Who the fuck is Nino Fallacci?

MARIA. My soul mate!!

ANGELA. Maria!?

VICTORIO. Angela this may not be the best time…

> (**ANGELA** *starts to go into a panic attack and needs to sit.* **OFFICER GARDNER** *storms in.*)

KELLY. We have an ambulance!

ANGELA. Perfect timing!

KELLY. I have Officer Frizalone holding down a path on Hylan Boulevard to clear her to Staten Island North. I have room for one more in the ambulance.

ANGELA. I'm coming! I hope you have drugs on the ambulance!

KELLY. They will take good care of your daughter.

ANGELA. I meant for me!

> (**ANGELA** *goes out and the* **OFFICER** *and* **JOSEPHINE** *and* **VICTORIO** *help* **MARIA** *and the baby out. The* **OFFICER** *takes the baby and they exit.*)

TONIANN. Anthony did you know about this Nino?

ANTHONY. Of course!

TONIANN. And you didn't tell me!?

ANTHONY. You have a big mouth!

TONIANN. I do not!

JOSEPHINE. Is he nice!? Does he have a job!?

ANTHONY. He's young. Starving actor. Cute though.

TONIANN. Oh perfect, just what she needs!

JOSEPHINE. Well at least he's Italian.

VICTORIO. Olivia, can we talk inside?

OLIVIA. Victorio, I think we have said all there is to say tonight.

VICTORIO. I still need to explain to you why...

OLIVIA. You don't need to explain anymore Victorio.

VICTORIO. I'm confused...

OLIVIA. I know. That's why I need to let you go.

ANTHONY. Olivia please...

OLIVIA. No Anthony, Victorio found something with you that I can't give him. It's not his fault and it's not your fault. It happens. It sucks but it happens and we are all going to get through this.

JOSEPHINE. Cause you're a Bianco! You're a fighter!

TONIANN. Josephine mind your business!

JOSEPHINE. That's my cousin!

FONZINA. Cousin?!

ANTHONY. Don't ask!

FABIANA. I'm so confused.

> (**OFFICER GARDNER** *storms through the door.*)

KELLY. I have room for one more in my emergency vehicle.

> (*To* **OLIVIA**.*) Sweetie you need to get out of here?

OLIVIA. I thought you would never ask!

> Good luck...to all of you.

TONIANN. We will see you soon I hope.

JOSEPHINE. You're family!

OLIVIA. I need a week alone in Saint Barts to figure this out. Victorio, I'll send you the bill. Come on officer... any bars open on the way to Dongan Hills?

KELLY. Muldoon's is open all night! Want to stop in for a holiday spirit?

OLIVIA. I thought you would never ask!

KELLY. Recently divorced.

OLIVIA. PERFECT! We will have a lot in common!

KELLY. Merry Christmas Everyone!!!

(They exit.)

TONIANN. Come on everyone, why don't we give the boys some time alone.

JOSEPHINE. I want to hear this.

TONIANN. You nosey fuck, let's go.

FABIANA. I'm still so confused!!

JOSEPHINE. Come on sisters I'll explain the whole story!

TONIANN. The bullshit version!

FABIANA. You got Sambuca!?

FONZINA. Scotch!

JOSEPHINE. My kind of nuns! Merry Christmas!!

(They all exit leaving **ANTHONY** *and* **VICTORIO** *alone on stage.)*

VICTORIO. You've been quiet.

ANTHONY. What do you want me to say Victorio?

VICTORIO. How do you feel?

ANTHONY. Upset, confused, relieved...this is A LOT.

VICTORIO. Well I only feel one thing right now, FREE!

ANTHONY. I'm happy for you. I'm even happier for Olivia.

That poor woman lived in the dark for twenty years and you let her!

VICTORIO. Anthony, not all of us come from families like yours.

I grew up in a very catholic family. We had different beliefs and my family was very strict. If my Dad was alive and knew I was gay, well let's just say that news alone would of killed him before the cancer did.

ANTHONY. You could have told Olivia.

VICTORIO. I could have...

ANTHONY. How can I ever trust you again Victorio?

VICTORIO. What does your heart say Anthony?

ANTHONY. My heart is what always gets me in trouble.

VICTORIO. Okay well if you don't want to listen to me and you don't want to listen to your heart, then listen to everything that happened tonight. Your niece was born, my ex-wife is your cousin, nuns are in your kitchen right now. I mean what do you say to all that?

ANTHONY. Typical holiday.

VICTORIO. If we can overcome this Anthony, we can overcome anything.

ANTHONY. Good point.

VICTORIO. So we still going to Aruba Tuesday?

(**ANTHONY** *hesitates a moment then the nuns come out.)*

FABIANA. Forgive him you stupid ass!

FONZINA. What's the matter with you!?? A gorgeous Italian doctor!

FABIANA. Hey! If he doesn't go to Aruba I'll go!

(*They exit.)*

ANTHONY. Well I guess if they forgive you...

VICTORIO. Merry Christmas Anthony!

ANTHONY. Merry Christmas Victorio...

(**VICTORIO** *takes* **ANTHONY***'s hand and* **ANTHONY** *slowly lets him. A bitter sweet but emotional moment.* **ANTHONY** *finally allows the moment to happen and they embrace. They make eye contact and* **VICTORIO** *goes in to kiss* **ANTHONY** *and just as they do the lights go down and Christmas music swells up*.)*

(Christmas curtain call.)

---

* A license to produce MY BIG GAY ITALIAN CHRISTMAS does not include a performance license for any third-party or copyrighted music. Licensees should create an original composition or use music in the public domain. For further information, please see Music Use Note on page 3.